The Earl
of
Glamford

The Earl
of
Glamford

MICHAEL REDMOND

ARCHWAY
PUBLISHING

Archway Publishing books may be ordered
through booksellers or by contacting:

Archway Publishing
1663 Liberty Drive
Bloomington, IN 47403
www.archwaypublishing.com
844-669-3957

Interior Image Credit: Katherine Hickman

ISBN: 978-1-6657-4865-0 (sc)
ISBN: 978-1-6657-4866-7 (e)

Library of Congress Control Number: 2023915494

Print information available on the last page.

Archway Publishing rev. date: 09/05/2023

CONTENTS

Introduction.. ix

Chapter 1   A Disappearing Act.................................... 1
Chapter 2   The Glamford Ball 4
Chapter 3   In the Office of Sir Percival.......................14
Chapter 4   M. Archambeau...18
Chapter 5   New Years at Kirby's 24
Chapter 6   A Conspiracy Revealed 32
Chapter 7   Of Pirates and the Burglary 43
Chapter 8   Thoughts Regarding a Spiral Sliced Ham 48
Chapter 9   The Warning 53
Chapter 10   The Frenchman's Departure 57
Chapter 11   Uncle Roger's Secret................................ 62
Chapter 12   Help Comes in a Tweed Suit..................... 67
Chapter 13   The Secret Room 73
Chapter 14   The East End.. 76

Epilogue.. 83
Characters of Fiction... 85
Characters of History.. 87

Detective Archambeau

INTRODUCTION

A dark, windless October night in 1888. The patter of rain on the roofs. A cat meows in an alley, then runs off, the figure of a man is revealed as he steps into the light of a gas streetlamp. The man, dressed in a trench coat, looks both ways as he tentatively crosses the empty street. From within his coat, he takes a small package with a hellish letter and sets it on the steps of one of the houses. The crack of lightning and thunder! The man is gone. Gone into the rain. Gone into the winding streets. Gone into history.

CHAPTER I

A Disappearing Act

Now, our story begins among the throngs and workhouses of late 19ᵗʰ century London. Also encompassing the entirety of the isle of England and Wales in the Victorian era. We begin our tale, and follow an immensely wealthy factory owner by the name of Richard Goodborn...

Richard Goodborn was just as his last name suggested. He was born into a wealthy family, and he was brought up to appreciate the finer things in life. The catch is, however, that he did not seem to appreciate the so-called lesser things. Mr. Goodborn ran the largest factory corporation in London. He was respected, admired, and above all, feared. Along with the factory, he secretly ran the back-alley gambling dens, and was a force of destruction to the other tycoons of the upper class. Mr. Goodborn was powerful, but on the night of 22 December 1891, he was never heard from again...

For weeks and months after that fateful event, people

gossiped and speculated on the mysterious disappearance of the great and terrible Goodborn. His absence meant that there were now multiple people of wealth and luxury who were after control of the factory. But even more unsettling was the fact that the taverns and gambling houses were now going unchecked. Amidst this silent battle for supremacy and ownership of Goodborn Enterprises, two names emerged…

The first was a man of nearly equal importance. A man who had had his eye on Goodborn Enterprises for a long while. A man by the name of Charles Droves. Droves, unlike Goodborn, started from the bottom of society. He started at a linens factory when he was a boy, and quickly rose through the ranks. He soon rose to the job of vice chairman of the company, and that's when his real talents came into play. Charles Droves was, in no other way, a savvy and ruthless businessman. He cut ties with the weak and rubbed elbows with the dukes and barons of the aristocracy. He knew when to make a move, and when to stay quiet. He knew when to bluff, and when to fold. He was, consequently, the chief rival of the unfortunate Mr. Goodborn. The two factories, both producing clothing and linens, were within a block of each other. The two businessmen had been consumed in their competition, each man dedicated to making the linens from his factory more cheaply and more lavishly than that of his opponent. Now, however, Droves often found himself thinking that he should have retired several years earlier. He was no longer a spry young man, although his mind was as sharp as ever.

Our second competitor (although he did not know he would become one) is none other than one of the many aristocratic figures to come in contact with Droves. Lord Alexander Horatio Shaftesbury III, the 17th Earl of Glamford, and in familial possession of the Seven Isles. He had inherited his massive fortune, and only slightly less massive title from the oldest member of the family, Lord Horatio Shaftesbury. As a result of this long and glorious lineage, Alexander was the essence of what it is to be an aristocrat. Luxury, class, wealth, charm, and chivalry. He was the quintessential aristocrat. Always dressed in the latest fashion, and always in remarkably good standing with the well-to-do figures whom he often crossed paths (such is the life of a royal). Fabulously wealthy, and with dastardly good looks, the third of the illustrious line of A.H. Shaftesburys seemed, in the most humble and inconsequential opinions of you and I, to have everything a young aristocrat should want. Although he was but a handsome young man of 23, he often found himself bored with the lavish life in which he had been raised and dreamed of traveling and going on great adventures. But so far, he has been confined to England, the island he calls home. After all, the young earl spent his childhood locked away in Glamford, learning the finer things in life. While Alexander learned pristine manners, painting, piano and how to run an estate, all he wished for was to be out on grand adventures like his late father before him.

CHAPTER II

The Glamford Ball

Glamford Castle, home of Lord Shaftesbury, had been the chief landmark of the area around Glamford since the Second Crusade. It was a small castle in comparison to that of Burg Eltz or Carcassonne, and yet still proved to be an impressive architectural feat. The castle was a great fortified house with stone walls surrounding it, and a round tower on each side in front. The castle itself had undergone changes with each generation of Shaftesburys adding their own flavor. It was a great stone manor house with a fountain in front, and gardens in the back. The manor house had been improved upon by adding a round stone tower on one corner. In this longtime home of the Shaftesburys, Lord Shaftesbury was to hold the annual Glamford Christmas ball. Consequently, Glamford Castle was adorned with the most dazzling and dizzying decor. Holly and pine, Christmas trees and gifts, and above all, on the crest of the ballroom's crystal chandelier was placed a golden bough of special magnificence.

On the eve of the birth of the Christ child, the atmosphere surrounding Glamford Castle was grand. The housekeeper, maids, butler, chef, cooks, and footmen all bustled about in somewhat of an organized frenzy. Although the ballroom was the centerpiece of the castle, the dining hall was indeed the focal point of the party. It was soon to be filled with the most opulent, luxurious, and powerful individuals in all of Europe. The extended table in the center of the beautiful dining hall was set with the finest Ming Dynasty china and the most painstakingly handcrafted silverware. Exquisitely ornate silver chalices were filled with a superb 1874 Bordeaux.* The butler's pantry and buffet table along the dining hall wall overflowed with the masterful concoctions of Chef René DuBlanc, better known as Remmy.

Remmy was initially hired by Lord Shaftesbury due to the time Remmy prepared a pheasant so meticulously that the aroma of the prized fowl caused Shaftesbury to claim that just to be within the environment of such a meal had filled his stomach already. Remmy had previously grown up and lived in France. In Paris itself, to be more specific. When Remmy was a boy, his father was the town baker. He was practically born with a ladle in his hand. Ironically, the portly perfectionist was never without his trusty ladle. The same ladle he used to stir his still-yet-to-be-perfected secret ingredient soup. And if a sous chef was dawdling even a few seconds with their order, they would likely feel the crack of the ladle on their lazy skulls (a feeling one does not wish to experience more than once).

As Chef René was bustling out of the kitchen, at quite a trot mind you, he ran smack into Lord Shaftesbury!

"Oh pardon, Monsieur, I was just taking zis trey of Welsh Rabbit to zis table." said Remmy.

"You shant worry even a trifle, Remmy. By the way, is everything on schedule so far?"

"Oui absolumont, M'Lord! Except you might want to check in with zis butler. He has requested your presence to discuss a slight hiccup in zis guest list."

"Ah, thank you Remmy! I shall see to it immediately!" replied Alexander.

Alexander hurried down to the butler's pantry. Walter Billingsby had been serving the Shaftesburys since Alex's grandfather, Lord Periwinkle Horatio Shaftesbury, was in charge. Billingsby was as old as the hills but had looked around seventy-five years of age for quite some time. The townsfolk speculated that he was over 100 years old. Some say that during one of his annual month-long vacations, he had found the famed Fountain of Youth. As Alexander reached the butler's pantry, Billingsby informed the former of the situation.

"My Lord, it seems we have a late addition to our guest list. One that I think warrants your examination and approval."

Alexander glanced at the guest list, and noticed an unfamiliar name at the bottom, written, it seemed, in great haste. As if the butler had been under great duress when he wrote it down. He nodded his assent. There were many people attending this evening whom he did not know personally.

Finally, the old grandfather clock in the great hall (rumored to be crafted from magic wood of the tree grown from a seed of Newton's famous apple) struck the sixth hour of the afternoon. This clock carried not only the supposed history of gravity within its ornate details, but it was also observed by some to have never needed its hands reset. The only setting of its silver and gold hands to be recalled was when it was made for Alexander's great-great grandfather, Lord Alexander Horatio Shaftesbury II. Lord Alexander Horatio Shaftesbury II had been gifted this storied furnishing by the last surviving publisher of Newton's book on gravity. Nevertheless, the hour was that of unignorable import; for the 6 o'clock hour marked the official start of the Christmas party.

The first to arrive was none other than Madame Gertrude Plum. Madame Plum was the daughter of a French dignitary and even though she had married an English businessman, still insisted on being referred to in the French manner of madame. She was indeed the town gossip. Madame Plum was a rotund, ancient widow who frittered away her time having tea with her widowed friends and discussing the latest scandal. Totally scatter-brained, she had an annoying habit of batting her eyes when she spoke. Needless to say, the sole reason for her invitation was due to polite convention. To exclude a neighbor of her station and financial status would have been discourteous. After Madame Plum arrived, the other guests began pouring in. Dukes and duchesses, counts and countesses, barons, ladies and business tycoons. They came from every corner of the country and European continent.

Soon, all were seated at the great table. At the head of this enormous table was none other than Alexander himself. To his right, the Governor of the British colony in South Africa, Governor Arthur Royce. Arthur Royce was a man of zest. Of zeal. Arthur always favored a tweed suit, even on a formal occasion like this evening. This evening in honor of the Christmas holiday he donned a deep scarlet bow tie. With graying hair and great mutton chops, he always seemed to be on the hunt for the latest item of value and antiquity. He had, as a young man many years ago, led an expedition to Africa, and became absolutely captivated by the continent. In his old age, his love of fine food had added to his waistline, and he had become quite eccentric, and (as Madame Plum told anyone who would listen) a bit cracked in the head. The exuberant, story-telling governor was obsessed with collecting artifacts and displaying them in his great manor house in Glamford. The lovely old home had become a museum of sorts. Governor Royce had been a father figure to Alexander ever since Alexander's father passed away.

As they began the first course, the ever-boisterous Royce exclaimed, "Alexander, dear boy! How were things in Glamford while I was away?"

Alexander informed him, "Very well, Arthur. And tell me, how was your trip to Egypt? I trust you didn't get into any mischief this time?"

"My dear boy! It was MARVELOUS! I had a very

peaceful vacation. NOTHING like my trip to Cairo ten years ago!"

Alexander, (recognizing that the governor was about to launch himself into a wild tale about his travels) entertained his wish and made a face that affected disbelief mixed with just enough feigned curiosity to get the governor going.

"Oh yes," said the governor, believing he now had Alexander on the edge of his seat, "It was near ten years ago, in 1881, I believe. I got down there alright. Took a train from Morocco. And when I arrived in Cairo, everything seemed to be in order, but by George it was NOT!"

"Oh?" replied Alexander, who was leaning in with amusement.

"No. A strange man approached me. An American by the name of Klaus Obermier."

Alexander stifled a chuckle.

"This Klaus fellow said that he recognized me from my picture in the paper from last year. Remember that ridiculous escapade I was involved in with that insufferable prince from Damascus? Well, anyway, he told me that he was leading an expedition in Cairo. He told me he and his team had traced the location of a hidden store of gold to Egypt. Gold that once belonged to Mansa Musa, the great king of Mali, who it is said, would ruin the economies of entire nations due to his immense wealth! He would travel on his grand caravan across the desert to trade salt, and he would simply throw enormous amounts of gold to the citizens of whichever town he happened upon, which would inflate economies into utter collapse! Isn't that just FASCINATING, dear boy? Isn't it just GRAND?!"

The governor's story was interrupted by the arrival of the next course, which was roast duck, garnished with herbs and cooked to perfection under the watchful eye (and brandished ladle) of Remmy. As the second course was served, the conversation inevitably shifted to the events of December 22.

"I do say," said Governor Royce, "our esteemed colleague Mr. Goodborn has, in my weighty opinion, been kidnapped! Held for ransom no doubt!"

"PREPOSTEROUS!" roared a voice from the other end of the table.

This voice belonged to Charles Droves. Droves was sitting bolt upright in his chair as he continued his fuming tirade.

"It is MY opinion, Governor Royce, that Mr. Goodborn was assassinated! For after I heard the news of his disappearance, I had my son, Vincent, rush up to his estate in the Cotswolds. To our joint surprise he found a note on the floor of Goodborn's bedroom!"

A hushed silence drew over the dining hall.

"And just WHAT proof of demise did this note provide you?" countered Royce, who's face had turned from pink to scarlet.

"Do you DOUBT my word, Governor?!" said Droves.

"Indeed, I do! There is no such letter!" retorted Royce.

"You are sadly mistaken, sir! For this note that my son found was written in the hand of Goodborn himself! And what's more, the letter alludes to the fact that Goodborn KNEW someone would murder him!"

"IRRELEVANT TWADDLE!" Royce exclaimed. "I

tell you sir, Mr. Goodborn is still alive! I refuse to believe that he was simply murdered with nothing to show for it! Show me the letter, you babbling fool!"

At this point, Alexander interjected, and told the two that they could settle their differences elsewhere.

After dinner, the guests migrated to the ballroom. Alexander hated dancing, but as a noble, he was required to dance at a formal event like this. The people were mingling and chatting when Alexander heard a voice behind him.

"Alexander, dear boy, I must apologize for my childish behavior at the table this evening. But I must also tell you that Charles Droves is a cheat, I tell you! A cheat!"

"Calm down, Arthur. Enjoy the party!" said Alexander.

"Well, I don't see you in a hurry to get out on the dance floor," said the governor. "I have observed that a certain young lady has indeed been trying to catch your eye tonight."

"Oh, nonsense Arthur! Nothing of the sort!" replied Alexander, trying to change the subject.

"Come on, you stubborn boy!" coaxed Royce, as he shoved Alexander into the fray where Alexander bumped into the subject of the previous conversation.

Princess Romina Casanova, a beautiful woman of 21, was 7th in line for the throne of Tsar Alexander III (although she would never get a chance at the throne, because in November of 1894, the last Tsar of all of Russia would succeed Alexander III). She wore a glimmering silver ball gown that glowed nearly as much as her lovely face. Alexander's face promptly turned a deep, reddish hue as he tried to politely and gracefully escape the situation.

Alexander was not at all short of charm or chivalry when in the presence of women, but to be in the presence of the princess rendered all his charm null and void, as he found himself very much caught off guard.

"But where are you going, Alexander?" questioned Princess Romina.

Alexander, knowing he must maintain class and etiquette on occasions like this, reluctantly turned back to face this mysterious, and beautiful princess. Making a small bow, he took her hand and led her to the dance floor.

"How did you know my name?" asked Alexander.

"Because I heard that man talking to you, and your name was on the invitation."

What an idiot! How stupid I must seem! thought Alexander, chastising himself.

"Of course, how silly of me to forget. Yes, that is Governor Arthur Royce, who is something of a godfather to me. He was informing me of his latest adventure in Cairo."

"It must be wonderful, to travel! I've always wanted to travel extensively and hope to eventually visit America! You must tell me about your many adventures some time," the princess said with a smile.

Alexander, in fact, had rarely traveled abroad. Hardly outside of England. Hardly even outside of Glamford. But he mustn't appear to be a child to the likes of Princess Romina.

"Oh yes of course! I have gone on a few adventures of my own, in fact."

Dear God, what am I doing! thought Alexander.

"So, you have been to America? You must tell me all about it!" Romina exclaimed with childlike glee.

Alexander had never been to America. He had learned basic history in his schooling as a child, but there was no way he could even pretend to know what he was talking about.

"Well, you see…"

Alexander was about to begin telling the princess the truth, but before he had the chance, a hand came down on the back of his jacket collar, and he was pulled back, and off the dance floor!

CHAPTER III

In the Office of Sir Percival

The owner of the hand spun Alexander around! The hand belonged to none other than Governor Royce, who seemed terribly distressed!

"Shhhh! You must come with me! Quickly!" Royce hissed.

Alexander excused himself and followed his troubled godfather down a dark, little used passageway into an empty office. The office was a dimly lit room with grey stone walls and a grand fireplace etched into the middle of the back wall. In it were two leather lounge chairs and a great mahogany desk. The entirety of the room was surrounded by books of every subject. The room, now used as a library, had once been Alexander's father's office.

Sir Percival Horatio Shaftesbury was, much like Arthur Royce, an adventurer. He and Arthur, as young men, used this room to plan their next trip and talked of treasures and great wild places. They were best friends. Alexander's father had gone on many adventures with the old governor. They saved each other's lives on quite a few occasions. Above the great desk was a grand portrait of Sir Percival. The room had been left virtually untouched since his untimely death.

Then, pale as a ghost, Governor Royce relayed his harrowing findings.

"Alexander, come close. You must listen to me! After dinner, Charles Droves approached me. He seemed extremely agitated! He said he was too old for this sort of thing. He shoved something into my hand in a rush to get rid of it, as if it were a hot coal, and told me to give it to you!"

From within his tweed suit, the frightened governor produced a letter, and with a shaking hand, gave it to his godson. Alexander took it as if the letter were his own child and gingerly opened it. It read:

To The Bearer of This Letter,

> *My name is Richard H. Goodborn. I own and oversee my company, Goodborn Enterprises. Over the last month, I have received threats to my life. I sincerely believe someone is pursuing me. Be it for my money, my company, or for a personal matter I do not know. But whosoever obtains this letter, know this: I feel a heavy weight upon my heart of late. As if shackles are chained to my very soul. I cannot escape this terrible dread. It is not long now. Last week I received a letter with no address. The sender did not provide any information about himself. It was written*

*in some sort of ghastly red ink. I fear that this
letter may be my last, which is why I shall
inform you of the secret within Uncle Roger.
There you will find another letter. I may be
able to avenge my death, with your help, from
within my predestined grave.*

*Sincerely,
Richard Harold Goodborn
21 December 1891*

Alexander slowly handed the letter back to Royce and dropped into one of the lounge chairs. The mysterious and ominous nature of the letter had sent the two into a daze. Each contemplating their own theories. The governor was pacing back and forth around the room with that adventurous glimmer in his eye, which usually meant trouble.

"There is but one thing to do. We must find that note! And we will start by going to Goodborn's estate in the Cotswolds!" announced Royce.

Suddenly, Alexander thought he saw something flashing by the window. In his recently heightened state of alert (due to the nature of the letter), he leapt out of the chair and dashed towards the window, just in time to see a figure disappear into the trees that surround that corner of the castle. Alexander jumped out of the window and over the stone balustrade. Much to the governor's great surprise, he watched Alexander run at full chat towards the woods! The excitable Royce nearly jumped out of the window himself, but remembered just in time that he was not a young lad anymore, and subsequently made his way to the door as quickly as he dared. He bustled down the hallway, where the party was still in full swing, and ducked and dodged his way closer to the outside door. Suddenly he ran into Charles Droves, who dropped his slice of Christmas pudding into the hands of Royce, who juggled it for a moment, lost his balance, and fell to the floor, taking Droves with him!

"My word! Just where are you going in such a hurry!" Droves exclaimed with profound annoyance.

"Move! You monochromatic philistine!" countered Royce, who brushed himself off, and continued his interrupted dash for the door.

Once Royce finally got himself outside, he saw Alexander covered in mud and dirt, heading his way.

"I couldn't find him!" gasped Alexander, out of breath. "I saw someone run past the window and into the woods. He must have been listening in on us, but for what reason?"

As the pair made their way back to Sir Percival's office, they drew the surprised gasps and wonderment of the guests who had congregated near the entrance; each giving his or her feeble attempt of pretending to be deeply interested in each other's conversations. Once the two had gotten back to the office, a look of shock eclipsed their faces. Goodborn's letter was gone!

CHAPTER IV

M. Archambeau

Two days later, as the sun rose and lit up the beautiful rolling hills and little woods of Glamford Castle, Alexander and Governor Royce were preparing to set out for the Cotswolds. Governor Royce was understandably in a bit of fog that morning after the shock at the party. Alexander was enjoying his breakfast of scotch eggs and kedgeree when the stableboy entered the room and meekly informed him that the carriage was ready. Finishing their breakfast, they got into the waiting chaise. The open-top, two-seater was driven by their coachman, Samuel Brown, (who was a former slave hired by Alexander to tend to the stables and carriages) and was led by two tremendous Clydesdale horses named Fred and Sneeze. Thus began their journey to Mr. Goodborn's Cotswolds residence.

After a long journey (and a few rests for the horses) the party arrived at Mr. Goodborn's estate. Made from traditional stone, and with a stone-tiled roof, the house was just what one would expect in the Cotswolds area. When Alexander approached the door, he saw that it was ajar. He cautiously stepped inside (with Royce following behind). The house was furnished as if Goodborn had just gone outside for a walk. Nothing seemed disturbed or out of place.

"Do you remember what that letter said?" questioned Royce.

"I only remember that he was terribly frightened and mentioned something about his Uncle Roger." Alexander replied.

The pair continued to wander around the empty house. Alexander went upstairs and found himself in Goodborn's bedroom. The bedroom of Mr. Goodborn was indeed rumored to be the scene of the crime. Yet, there was not a book out of place, nor a wrinkle in the neatly made bed sheets. There was not a fraction of evidence that would lead one to believe that this upper room of a humble cottage house in the English countryside was the scene of a grisly murder. The governor and his godson continued to search the house. Royce searched the cellar, while Alexander carried on his examination of the top floors. Alexander opened the door to Goodborn's study, and there, above the desk, was a portrait of a man. This man was depicted in an officer's uniform and sported a mustache and a monocle. The painting was titled: Lt. Roger Goodborn, 1861.

Alexander was about to yell for Royce, when he heard the click of a pistol being cocked behind him.

"Not a sound, monsieur." said the voice behind him. "Please take the painting off the wall, good sir."

Alexander did as he was told.

"If I may," said Alexander, "I would like to know just who is ordering me to do his bidding?"

The man with the gun replied, "I am positively sure you have heard of me. I am only the greatest detective in all of France! For I, monsieur, am known as Inspecteur Gerard Archambeau!"

Alexander was taken aback. As the young man was taking the painting down, he wondered to himself what this mysterious Frenchman was doing in the cottage of Mr. Goodborn and threatening a young aristocrat no less! Alexander turned around slowly to give the detective the painting and saw that M. Archambeau was dressed even more lavishly than he. Archambeau wore what must have been the finest suit in all of Paris, which was custom fitted by undoubtedly the finest tailor in all of Paris as well. He had a brilliant pointy mustache and wore a magnificent wide brimmed hat, which kept his flowing brown hair at bay. The inspector was also carrying a second pistol of the same make as that which was aimed at Alexander. Two French-made ivory handled revolvers.

"There doesn't seem to be anything in the backing of the painting." Alexander informed his captor.

"You will be accompanying me to my carriage, good sir." the inspector beckoned.

"I don't believe he will be assisting you after all," interjected Royce, who was standing behind the startled inspector, and holding his trusty revolver to the back of Archambeau's head.

"Quite clever, monsieur, I must admit," the inspector remarked. "I should have checked the cellar, and now look where my carelessness has gotten me. Well played, sir, well played indeed. But if you had considered the possibility that I may also have traveled with an accomplice, you would have entered with a much greater degree of caution. But alas! The thought must not have crossed your mind! If it had, you may have noticed that the front door was ajar when you arrived, and you must also have realized that evidence is key to solving any sort of crime. AND," continued the detective, "you must also have realized that a clever investigator such as myself would not touch the subject of a very revealing letter with his bare hands. So, I simply waited for this young man to find the painting, so that it could be removed from the wall, and at the same time remain untouched by capable, and I will admit, stupidity un-gloved hands."**

Archambeau, with lightning reflexes, drew his second pistol and pointed it at the governor!

"Now, you see, I have the upper hand! I now have the privilege, nay, the PLEASURE of blowing both of your empty skulls back to Glamford! Ah yes," remarked the detective, who noticed the bewilderment on the governor's face, "It was I who stole the letter from under your very noses! And it was I who was hired by an unnamed personage to capture the killer of Richard Goodborn!"

A shot fired from the stairwell glanced off the stone wall and landed inches from Alexander's face! Royce took advantage of the distraction and swept the Frenchman from under his feet. Alexander made a dash down the stairs with the painting still in hand! The man who fired the shot was the driver of Monsieur L'Inspecteur's coach. Alexander and Royce ran outside, leapt into their carriage and sped away as fast as Fred and Sneeze could carry them.

Archambeau was not far behind. His carriage, led by faster chargers, was gaining on them. The two carriages were soon side-by-side, and the inspector and the governor were shooting at each other! The driver of the inspector's carriage jumped off his perch and tackled poor Samuel Brown to the ground! The two carriages rattled on, and the passengers inside continued their skirmish, completely unaware of the circumstances outside. As the two carriages were careening down the road, Archambeau's two horses started to overtake the exhausted Clydesdales, but not before Archambeau leapt onto Alexander's carriage! He landed between his two adversaries, snatched the painting off the floor, and jumped off the carriage within a matter of seconds!

Alexander quickly climbed up front and turned his horses around, but he was too late! Archambeau was nowhere in sight! A short distance further back, Royce spotted the two drivers. They were not locked in a heated struggle as one would expect but conversing amicably about who they thought got away with the painting. Archambeau's loyal driver was a man by the name of Pierre DuMont. DuMont began his career as a jockey for the illustrious Rothschild family in France. Two broken legs and his devil-may-care attitude, however, got him sacked. His love of excitement, gambling and unpredictability were well satisfied in Archambeau.

As the two looked up at the empty-handed Alexander and the frazzled Royce, Samuel reluctantly handed his money over to DuMont, who smugly accepted his winnings. Then the three companions set off back to Glamford while DuMont headed for a tavern in town, eager to make more profit off his winnings.

CHAPTER V

New Years at Kirby's

Two days passed, and Alexander and Royce were still puzzled over what happened. Who was this mysterious Frenchman, Archambeau? Who had hired him to find the killer, and why? All these questions, dear reader, are soon to be answered, but as we return to Glamford Castle, we see the butler, Billingsby, giving a letter to Alexander at breakfast that morning. Written in elaborate script, the letter read:

Lord Alexander H. Shaftesbury III,

I most cordially extend to you an invitation to a New Year's Eve celebration. The dress shall be formal. Please arrive no earlier than 6:00 p.m. I would be honored with your presence at such an event. The party shall be held at 7 Riversdale Rd, Liverpool,

*England. Safe travels, and a happy New Year
to you and your family!*

*Your Most Humble Servant,
J. Kirby Amsworth*

Alexander read the letter once more, and then put it in his pocket. After he was finished with breakfast, he told Samuel to get his horse ready. Alexander's horse was a black Cleveland Bay riding horse, named Moonlight.

Alexander rode to Royce's estate. Governor Royce's house was, as was mentioned earlier, a museum of sorts. With a fountain out front, and a well-maintained garden in back, one would think that the mansion in between was run with the same attention to detail. But one who assumed this would be mistaken. Inside, Royce's estate was a menagerie of pelts, exotic furnishings, encyclopedias, tusks, trophies, and volumes upon volumes of books covering every possible aspect of the African continent. Alexander, who always had everything in perfect order at Glamford Castle, avoided his godfather's place like the plague. On this day, however, he braved the chaos, and stepped inside.

Alexander looked around, taking in the mess. The house looked as if it was used for storage, which it was, because the governor was in South Africa for an extended time during the year. But since he was in Glamford for the time being, he had once again taken up residence at Royce Hall. Alexander called out for the governor, but to no avail. Alexander started searching through the rooms of the old house and was amazed at what he found lying around! You must remember that Alexander had not been inside

Royce Hall in years. He saw animal heads with great fangs, many miscellaneous artifacts, and he saw cascades of books scattered about. One book in particular drew his attention. It appeared to be an ancient manuscript and was set to an open page in a glass case. The open page had a drawing of what looked like a crying baby curled up inside an open egg. Alexander continued to search the old house, and at one point stopped cold in his tracks, shocked at something else he found tucked away betwixt the mess. After a protracted hour or more of tedious sorting and dizzying seeking, he eventually realized that a further search would be pointless. Leaving a note with a witless hall boy, Alexander mounted Moonlight and returned to Glamford Castle, a little concerned and wondering where Royce could be.

The day of the new year's party arrived, and Alexander still had heard nothing from his unpredictable godfather. As Alexander entered his room to select his attire for the evening, he heard an unexpected bellow downstairs. The loud blustering belonged to the frenzied personage of Arthur Royce. Royce stormed up to Alexander's room, and in a terrible fit, burst through the door.

"The Battlecrease House?! Are you quite mad?!" exclaimed Royce.

Alexander matched the tone of the governor in his response, "The Codex of Leicester?! THE Codex?!"

Royce was taken aback, and answered haphazardly, "Oh yes…DaVinci…The notebook…" Royce returning to his senses explained, "DaVinci's notebook, better known as The Codex of Leicester. Yes, that is the one. I found it in a tomb under St. Mark's on my second trip to Venice, which must have been 20 or so years ago. It was buried with someone of great importance, but it was not the tomb of Leonardo DaVinci, which is what I was trying to find. But that doesn't matter. My question to you is why in God's name were you invited to a party at Battlecrease? You know what happened there! I don't like it! I say you shouldn't go!"

"That is just what I was going to say to you," replied Alexander. "I got a letter from a man named Kirby Amsworth, and he invited me, of all people, to a party tonight. I don't know why he would invite me, seeing as I have never met the man nor knew he existed for that matter."

"Well, I don't think you should go! We all know what happened to Mr. Maybrick! It was all over the papers! It's trouble, I tell you. That house…" warned Royce.

"What I would like to know is why anyone would buy that house, and so soon after what happened?" Alexander wondered. "And besides, it is too late, I have already decided to go. Mr. Amsworth seemed like a harmless fellow in his invitation. Maybe he was Maybrick's partner in his cotton business, or whatever he did for a living, I don't recall."

After donning his formal evening attire, Alexander bid farewell to Royce and Billingsby. He strode through the great hall and out the massive front door onto the wide drive where Samuel Brown was waiting with the bow fronted brougham. Once inside the elegant, highly lacquered carriage, he and Samuel set off for 7 Riversdale Road. By the time Alexander got to the infamous residence of Mr. Amsworth, the clouds had rolled in, and the sky had darkened, warning of a coming storm. The structure at 7

Riversdale Road was a great manor house. It was a pleasant looking, three-story home painted white with tall windows. Tucked behind trees and foliage it seemed unassuming. The dark clouds loomed ominously over the house. The neighbors told stories of strange noises in the night, and dark figures in the windows. But tonight, the old wives' tales were forgotten. No one spoke of what had happened at the house. Many people had already arrived, and as Alexander handed his Chesterfield coat, top hat and gloves to one of Mr. Amsworth's servants, he was greeted by the man himself, who acted as if he had known the 17th Earl of Glamford for years.

J. Kirby Amsworth was a well-established man with a receding hairline, a proud mustache, and coal like eyes. Without the privilege of a remarkable appearance, he was the sort that one would imagine managed a successful shop, or perhaps occupied a position at a local bank.

"Welcome, My Lord, to my humble abode! Your arrival has brought a smile to my face, as I surely thought a person of your stature (Amsworth winked) would have other plans on New Year's Eve. But fortune has smiled upon me tonight, as my New Year's Eve party has begun in all its splendor! But please, come in, come in, out of the dark night, and into the warmth and wonders of my party!"

Alexander thanked his host and took in his surroundings. Many people were standing around, conversing amongst themselves. In every room on the ground floor, people of the upper-middle class and beyond, were sharing news, gossiping, or relaying their recent adventures with old friends. Everybody seemed to know each other. Nothing seemed out of the ordinary. And yet, Alexander did not feel at ease. Instead, he felt an eerie sensation, as if a weight had been placed on his soul, much like that of visiting the grounds where a great battle had taken place many years ago. It felt as if the house itself was carrying a dark secret. Alexander was surprised to see people in such a merry mood. Surely, they had all heard about what happened here not so long ago. Suddenly, as if to confirm Alexander's inner thoughts, a boom of thunder marked the start of a deluge outside. It had been an uncharacteristically warm winter, bringing more rain than snow, especially for New Year's in England.

As Alexander made his way around the house, he didn't recognize many people. He was not expecting to hear anyone call his name, least of all the voice that belonged to Princess Romina. Alexander spun around, and to his surprise, there she was! The princess looked even more beautiful than when he met her at Christmas. This evening she wore a Worth ball gown of heavy crimson velvet. The fitted bodice was draped in an elaborate lace collar embroidered with tiny pearls. Her hair was swept up in a sophisticated style that showed off her lovely face and neck. She wore no jewelry other than tiny pearls in hair and upon her earlobes.

Alexander grinned despite himself and mentioned the absurd chances of the two meeting again at this particular party. The princess smiled and said that she had been staying in London since the Glamford Ball and received an invitation for this evening. Having nothing else to do and taking the invitation as a chance to see more of England, she accepted. The two were soon deep in conversation, and the once daunting atmosphere of the party dissolved into a most pleasant evening. Later, as the two were talking, Alexander was approached by Mr. Amsworth.

"Lord Shaftesbury, I see you have met Princess Romina! You two talk as if you have known each other for years, I couldn't help but overhear. Is that so?"

"We have previously met, but we are hardly more than acquaintances."

"Aah," Amsworth exclaimed understandingly, "Lord Shaftesbury, I hear a good deal about a Governor Arthur Royce in the paper every now and then. Is he perhaps your uncle? I thought I remembered hearing that he was your relation?"

"He is my godfather, Mr. Amsworth, and does seem to appear in the papers rather often," replied Alexander.

"I see. I must continue making the rounds, you know. Attend to my guests! I am glad you two are enjoying yourselves!" Amsworth turned to leave, but stopped, turned back and said, "And the house was left to me in the previous owner's will it seems. Oh, and no need for formalities! Call me Kirby!"

As Mr. Amsworth was leaving, Alexander was trying to figure out how his host seemed to answer his questions before he asked them.

The princess, as if reading Alexander's mind, exclaimed, "He is a peculiar fellow, but he seems harmless enough. He is probably just lonely in this great house all alone."

"I don't know..." Alexander's puzzled brow furrowed. "You notice how he seemed to know what I was thinking. And he acted as if we were old friends when I arrived."

"I certainly didn't know him before tonight, and he seemed to know me as only a loose acquaintance," said the Russian princess.

As the party went on through the evening, Alexander and the princess's friendship grew. The princess told Alexander about life in Russia, and that she too had been dreaming of traveling and going on marvelous adventures. It was only when people started leaving after the clock struck midnight that the pair realized that they had been talking for hours. As the party dissipated, the two friends said their goodbyes, and headed their separate ways. All was well in Alexander's world when Samuel Brown pulled up in the brougham. The young earl got in and rode back to Glamford in the rain and wind of the night.

CHAPTER VI

A Conspiracy Revealed

The month of January is usually a time of dismal cold after the holidays. One seems to want nothing more than for the sun to shine, and to see the grass again. But for Alexander, the month of January was wonderful. The princess had remained in England for a month after the New Year's party, and the two had spent almost every day together. It was the best time of Alexander's life. They frequently had lunch at Glamford Castle and went riding. Alexander on Moonlight, and the princess on one of Alexander's other horses: a tame white quarter horse named Zeke. The earl taught the princess to ride, and they had a marvelous time. However, every so often, Alexander felt that same eerie feeling he first felt at Mr. Amsworth's house. Yet, he shrugged it off, putting it out of his mind.

After the princess departed for Russia, Alexander settled back into his normal life, although he now had the privilege of writing to the beautiful, young woman. Two days after the princess left England, Alexander and Royce met in town for luncheon. They had not seen each other in weeks and the sight of the governor reminded Alexander of what he had seen tucked away at Royce Hall earlier.

"I do beg your pardon, but as I was searching for you last month before the party, I did indeed find the Codex, but even more astounding was what I found in the next room! It looked like a sarcophagus of some sort, and I have been wondering all this time if it had anything to do with the Egypt adventure you began telling me about on Christmas Eve?"

"Ah yes," Royce remembered, "my Egyptian trip of 1881. Well, I went to Cairo and met that Klaus fellow. And he told me about a project he and his team were working on. They thought they had found gold that once belonged to Mansa Musa, but after I agreed to join their expedition, I found out that they had been very much mistaken! It was the gold of Ahmose I! And we found the pharaoh himself along with it!"

"You're saying that the sarcophagus in your house contains the remains of a pharaoh?!" Alexander asked in shock.

"Oh no dear boy! It is merely the outside cover of the real sarcophagus and coffin. We sold the mummy to a prestigious museum in Germany. Although I will say that, along with the cover, I also made off with two sacred jars that were used to store Ahmose's organs. I had to smuggle them back to England! Klaus was not an American after all and wanted Germany to claim full ownership and notoriety for the findings, even though it was I who accidentally fell through a trap and found my way into the burial chamber! A pox upon foreign archaeologists!"

Just then, a boy approached and handed a note to Royce. The note read:

> *Meet me at my factory in London at 10 o'clock tonight. It is urgent.*
>
> *C.D*

After reading the note, Alexander and Royce looked around to see where the boy went, but he was gone.

That night, Royce and Alexander arrived at the entrance of Mr. Droves's factory, which was located near the London docks. The factory was a great brick building that blended perfectly with the surrounding area. The two decided to enter through the back entrance, which was a small door in the alleyway on the left side. They looked around and saw the factory's machines for threading and producing cloth and fabrics. Looking across the factory to the opposite wall, they saw a light in the room above. Alexander and Royce climbed the small, rickety stairway to the room and when they stepped inside, they saw Mr. Droves; and to their surprise, Inspector Archambeau! The crafty detective was dressed all in black and sitting in a chair to the left of Droves, who was seated at his desk.

"Gentlemen," Droves began, addressing the two compatriots, motioning them to be seated. "I have summoned you here tonight under the gravest circumstances. But let me enlighten you on the events of the past couple of months."

Droves lit his meerschaum pipe, leaned back in his

chair, and began to reveal his point of view on the recent events of the holidays. "Lord Shaftesbury, you may have noticed back in December, that a name was added to your guest list in haste. That name was mine. I invited myself to your party because I wished to give your friend here a note." Droves waved his pipe in the direction of Royce, who was listening with a look of mistrust on his face.

"The note which I had given to Mr. Royce contained a letter written by the late Richard Goodborn. As you know, the letter revealed Mr. Goodborn's situation just days before he vanished. Two days after Goodborn's disappearance, the London police came knocking on my door. They suspected ME of the MURDER of Mr. Goodborn, as part of some foul design to obtain Goodborn's business as my own! But may I convince you that, although I have in the past used…underhanded tactics to gain the financial edge over Goodborn, I would NEVER stoop so low as to commit murder!" Mr. Droves explained. With some exasperation he continued, "When I first received the letter, I hired Monsieur L'Inspecteur Archambeau to handle the case for me. I knew that one of you would try to find Uncle Roger and seeing as I can only trust the most prestigious detective to handle the only clue to the murder, I sent the best detective in all of France to recover it, which he did."

"He threatened to kill me!" Alexander exclaimed.

"A mere technicality of the profession, I am sure," Droves replied, "but let us set aside your unfortunate run in and I will tell you just why you are here."

"If I may," interjected Archambeau, who had been quite silent until now. He rose from his seat and paced the room, twisting his mustache. "The mention of Uncle Roger was not the only clue. If I recall correctly, Monsieur Goodborn noted that the letter of malice he received was written in, as he said, 'ghastly red ink'. Now, as a private investigator of the highest caliber and quality, I study all types of crime, in all places. With the clues in Goodborn's letter, I have made a quite worrying connection to the infamous happenings of a few years ago, not far from this factory."

"Surely not!" Royce said in disbelief. "He vanished years ago! The papers haven't had a story like that in the East End since '88! Why would that devil disappear for 3 and a half years, just to make a return in a completely different part of England?"

"Ah! I understand your well-founded doubt," said Archambeau, "however, I have been studying the case and narrowed my findings down to one theory: I believe the murders were committed by a man of a wealthier status. The police searched nearly every house in the Whitechapel area and found nothing concrete. Perhaps they were simply looking in the wrong location? This, my friend," the detective motioned to Alexander, "is why we need YOU! You are an aristocrat and therefore, would not look out of place at the formal events you will be attending. You must befriend this man, and gain his trust, and only then will the true nature of his character be revealed!"

"But who could you possibly suspect?" Alexander questioned.

"Why, you have already encountered him. Mr. James Maybrick, of 7 Riversdale Road, known to most as Battlecrease House."

"But Mr. Maybrick is dead! Poisoned with arsenic by his wife years ago. It was all over the papers!"

"That is exactly what he would like you to think!" said the detective triumphantly. "James Maybrick lives, but under a different name…or is it so different? The man who takes up residence at Battlecrease is Mr. J. Kirby Amsworth."

"Mr. Amsworth?! He seemed like a very pleasant host when I attended his New Year's Party. I don't understand. Do you mean to say that…"

"YES!" the inspector interrupted. "Maybrick and Amsworth are one and the same! My theory is this: Mr. Maybrick faked his death, and fled the country for several years, only to return as a distant relative named Kirby Amsworth. If you read the name backwards it reveals the hellish reality! J. Kirby Amsworth can be re-written in one word as Htrowsmaybrik J. A mere correction of the order and phonetics reveals J. Maybrik! With your help, the people of Whitechapel will finally rest well at night, you will be a national hero, and I will cement myself as the greatest detective in history! You are tasked with befriending Mr. Amsworth. You are tasked with befriending the devil himself! Jack the Ripper!"

In the following days, Alexander and Royce endeavored to learn everything they possibly could about the Whitechapel murders. Royce first went to the lavish estate of Madame Gertrude Plum, who over the years kept every newspaper she had ever read. Given her great girth, she remained seated when the housemaid escorted Royce into the drawing room where she was dealing with morning correspondence. Delighted to have a caller, especially an eligible male caller, she set aside her missive and gave the governor her full attention.

Over tea, Royce made his request to borrow her 1888 newspapers. She was somewhat suspicious of this odd request, especially from Royce of all people, but she agreed to let him borrow the newspapers covering the case. Hosting her ample body from the seemingly delicate mahogany desk chair, she escorted Royce through a labyrinth of hallways to the family muniment room. There among the legal documents, household ledgers, correspondence and business documents were mountains of old newspapers. Her librarian, familiar with every piece of paper in the room, quickly directed the governor to the stack of newspapers from 1888. A delighted Royce gathered the desired papers, thanked his hostess and made a hasty retreat before Madame Plum could detain him any further. Arriving home, he began his examination and did not re-appear for days.

Meanwhile, Alexander was learning all he could about Mr. Maybrick, and consequently, at the same time about Mr. Amsworth. Using his lofty social position, he gained knowledge through connections at the City of London Police, the Metropolitan Police (more commonly known for its location, Scotland Yard), as well as through Maybrick's old business colleagues. Try as he might, he couldn't find any information about Amsworth prior to his arrival at Battlecrease House shortly before Christmas. Alexander even sent Samuel Brown into Whitechapel to gain any information he could on the past crimes of The Ripper.

Alexander had dreamed of going on adventures like his godfather, and like his father had done years ago. But he now found it ironic that when he finally got a chance at adventure, the adventure was a bid at catching the most gruesome killer in history.

Between his studies and the responsibilities of a young earl, he wrote and received letters from the princess. She was intelligent and had a witty sense of humor, which kept him on his toes. Having gained one another's trust, they became the best of friends. The only thing Alexander refrained from mentioning was his assigned task, so as not to worry her.

The days passed, and each day, Alexander dreaded the inevitable second invitation from Mr. Amsworth. He usually succeeded in distracting himself by corresponding with Princess Romina or his voracious appetite for knowledge through books and research.

One day as the earl was reading in the conservatory, Royce stopped by. He was carrying a briefcase and was his usual excitable self. He led Alexander into Sir Percival's study. Once inside, he opened the briefcase and plopped down a massive folder. The folder contained every possible piece of obtainable evidence concerning the murders.

"Look here, dear boy! As you know, as of late I have been somewhat of a hermit. In my time I compiled newspaper stories, as well as researched the history and goings on of the Maybrick house. Enjoy!" The preoccupied Royce patted the folder. "Now I must leave you to catch up on the case by yourself. I have been summoned back to South Africa for a spell, which means you are on your own. Good luck, dear boy!"

"What? You can't just…" Alexander started to protest, but his friend was already gone.

Alexander was now on his own. Left to vanquish the great evil that had ravaged his homeland. Plus, he was one of only four men who suspected the truth. It had been over three years. Most thought the worst of it was over. But alas! The summit of evil, the faceless terror, the bane of London, The Ripper, had returned! And one man was tasked with jumping headlong into the lion's den! Alexander tried not to panic, and instead, thought of what he must do. Royce was gone. For a week? A year? This left only two men to consult: the ever-scheming Droves, and the ostentatiously astute M. Archambeau, neither of whom were completely in the trust of the young earl. But seeing as he had no other options, he wrote a letter to Droves inviting him and his accomplice to tea.

When the pair arrived at Glamford Castle, Alexander invited them around back to the conservatory overlooking the gardens. Here in the humid warmth of sunlit glass and exotic plants, they could see the lavish outdoor gardens (now mostly dormant in winter), enjoy their tea and discuss the dilemma. But before we listen in on their conversation, we must understand the pure magnificence of what was known as The Glamford Gardens:

Although the castle at Glamford had been around since medieval times, the gardens had not taken shape until Alexander's grandfather, Lord Periwinkle Horatio Shaftesbury, had begun planting what would become the most famous and envied garden in England. The current groundskeeper, Gordon Hammond, had apprenticed under the previous groundskeeper, as had the one before him. Hammond lived for the garden and conservatory. He was a wiry, middle-aged man with inexhaustible energy. He perpetually had dirt under his fingernails and brown patches on his knees. He worked tirelessly to perfect his domain but was easily distracted and flitted from one task to another, often leaving his original project to be completed the next time he was distracted. Gordon was most often seen trimming something, or cutting grass, or watering here, and planting there. Given his erratic approach to work, no one could accurately predict where he might be at any hour of the day.

A cobblestone pathway lined with arborvitae trees lead a visitor from the conservatory door into the extraordinary garden. A vine covered trellis marked the entrance to the garden itself. The pathway converged into a crossroads where a fountain anchored the center. Among the endless varieties of flowers, the walkway split the garden into four quadrants. One quadrant was filled with herbs. Another was filled with vegetables. The third consisted of fruit trees, and the fourth, nearest the woods, was left as it had been 100 years ago, with a precisely cut lawn, and a sitting area near an ancient oak tree.

Now we shall return to winter, and the conservatory, where Alexander and his two accomplices were about to be served tea and refreshments. Although the gardens were compromised due to the winter weather, the conservatory made up for it tenfold. The canopied greenhouse contained exotic plants, flowers, and more luxurious paraphernalia such as a small fountain and sparkling chandelier. Dismissing Hammond from his pruning and puttering, the gentlemen settled around the tea table to speak in private and enjoy their tea.

Droves seemed to be in a better mood than usual. M. Archambeau was dressed as usual in black, with one exception. Today, his wide-brimmed hat was topped off with two large feathers, one black, and the other dark red. Alexander explained the departure of his godfather and produced the folder in which lay the unsorted evidence compiled by the governor.

To Alexander and Droves' surprise the inspector, fabulously dressed as always, did not show the slightest notion of interest in the revelations contained within the folder. Instead, he raised his hand for silence, rose from his chair, and beckoned the other two inside. M. Archambeau led the two to Sir Percival's office.

He began pacing the room and examining the walls and bookshelves. After a time, he reached as if to remove a big red book from the shelf nearest the outer wall. The book, however, did not come off the shelf! Instead, the detective pulled the book toward himself while Droves watched in amazement. Suddenly, the bookshelf opened to reveal a hidden stairwell! The three men descended the spiral stone steps into a hidden room.

CHAPTER VII

Of Pirates and the Burglary

The hidden room, which lay below Sir Percival's office, was previously known to Alexander, who was well familiar with all the hidden passageways of the castle. However, he had forgotten about it until this moment. As Archambeau lit some candles, the contents of the room were revealed. Upon the walls were muskets, pistols, and sabers. There was a single wooden table in the center and a large chest in the corner. The room was a small, crude dugout bunker, which likens to that of a mineshaft. The room, known as the War Room, was constructed by one of the fouler relatives who shared the Shaftesbury name. This relative was the war-mongering Robert Clyde Shaftesbury, who, in the 1700's, terrorized the Caribbean!

Originally commissioned by King William III, to be a privateer and bring pirates to justice, the despicable Robert turned pirate, and began to commandeer the very ships he was sworn to protect! He was known in the Americas as

Red Robert, due to the bloodstained Union Jack that waved menacingly upon the mast! Robert never used a pirate flag, permitting his backstabbing surprise techniques to capture many Spanish treasure ships, as well as Her Majesty's English galleons and caravels. Unlike other pirates, he was not known for a particular ship. Upon seeing his vessel with no pirate flag, other captains believed he was just another merchant.

Many a loyal privateer was falsely accused of being Robert, and were mistakenly sent to the gallows, but the real Red Robert was never caught! At the height of his infamous notoriety, he had amassed a fortune in Spanish gold, and was wanted for an immense bounty in every port.

After Robert's pirating days were over, he began his warring ways in earnest. It was at this time that he built the secret room. He used this room to plant the first seeds (even though he died before the war began) of what would be the Seven Years War between England, her colonies and France, which lasted from 1756-1763.   At the time of his passing, Robert's only bequest was on a scrap of paper. It contained a secret code written in invisible ink, and a single sentence: "The Sun Doth Not Shine Upon Gold Ill-Gotten".

It was rumored long after, that the unbreakable code was the key to Robert's lost Spanish treasure. There was much speculation that the treasure was buried on one of the Shaftesburys' Seven Isles. Alexander's great-great grandfather, Lord Alexander Horatio Shaftesbury II, heard the story from his second cousin, whose father had been given the code by the dying Robert. Before Robert died, he may have given the boy's father a single key as well. Lord

Alexander Horatio Shaftesbury II had long searched for this treasure, but it was never found. The Shaftesburys tried to forget their unfortunate relation, and so Robert Clyde Shaftesbury's maniacal deeds were scarcely discussed.

As you now know the historical and familial significance of this hidden room, we shall look towards M. Archambeau as he begins his explanation:

"I have gathered you here in this room so that prying ears shall not impede our progress. I knew of this room after my last uninvited visit to the study but let us dispense with explanations. Gentlemen, allow me to enlighten you. As we know, during the height of Jack the Ripper's fame, he sent a package to the police which contained a letter allegedly sent 'from Hell ', and the kidney of one of his victims. This has led me to believe that The Ripper may have kept other such organs. So, if I may delve further into my sickening proposition, I would ask that we endeavor to find such organs and present them as evidence to finally catch this monster! I will need the help of each of you, and if I am completely honest, our attempt will probably end in failure. However, it is a noble quest, deserving of my attention, and that which even if I fail, will grant me a hero's recognition!"

Later that moonlit night, Archambeau's driver, DuMont, (who had indeed had the night of his life in the tavern last we saw him) dropped off his employer and the earl three blocks from Battlecrease House. Battlecrease House had an ominous reputation which was only heightened by the dark of the night. Alexander had taken a page from the inspector's handbook and was also dressed totally in black.

They approached the great house and put their plan into motion.

Alexander climbed a tree that was in front of the house so that he could keep watch. From this vantage point he could also see inside to the second floor. Meanwhile, Archambeau snuck around to the back door. Producing a ring of 20-30 keys from within his black coat, the crafty inspector tried different keys in an attempt to unlock the massive door. Monsieur L'Inspecteur heard a snuffling sound behind him. He cautiously looked over his shoulder to see two great hounds asleep in the yard! Just as he found the correct key and turned the lock, the dogs awoke and immediately bounded towards him! He leapt inside and managed to close the door, but not before a piece of his black coat had been ripped off by the bigger and nastier of the two dogs. The barking startled Alexander and he almost fell out of the tree!

The detective, who had ironically broken into his fair share of houses, had remained calm in this situation. As he was testing the floor and walls for weak spots, he spotted a staircase leading down to what must have been the cellar. Noting the staircase, he continued putting his weight on different floorboards and tiles throughout the house and combing the walls as he did in Sir Percival's study, until he was interrupted by a sudden cry from outside!

Once the dogs had settled, Alexander had an idea. While he was looking in at the second-floor window, he saw that his tree was just to the side of a balcony that led into what looked like a bedroom. Alexander debated whether he would be able to make the leap to the balcony. He finally decided that indeed he could. The earl climbed out onto the branch as far as he dared and prepared to make the jump!

Alexander barely made the jump and was hanging on to the balcony for dear life. His flaying about had gained the attention of the dogs, who were now waiting under the balcony for their prey to fall. Archambeau, surmising what had occurred from Alexander's cry, hurried to the kitchen, opened the ice box and took a ham, plus an apple for himself, and rushed out the door. The detective got the dogs' attention, and creating a distraction threw the ham away from the balcony, enabling Alexander to drop to the ground.

"You should be getting back to my carriage," the inspector suggested, clearly annoyed by the earl's incompetence.

Heeding his accomplice's advice, Alexander limped back to the coach as fast as his legs would carry him, while the inspector strode away in the opposite direction, nonchalantly eating his apple.

CHAPTER VIII

Thoughts Regarding a
Spiral Sliced Ham

A few days after the mishap, Alexander's long-awaited invitation arrived in the mail. Alexander opened the letter, and read:

> *The Lord Shaftesbury,*
>
> *My dear friend, it is with great hospitality that I extend an invitation to a gathering at 7 Riversdale Road to celebrate my birthday on March 2, at 6 o'clock in the evening. Formal dress is expected. I am looking forward to your attendance!*
>
> *Many Loquacious Serendipities,*
> *J. Kirby Amsworth*

The feeling of dread that Alexander had managed to dispel now came roaring back, as he prepared to bear the inescapable burden of befriending the hellacious Mr. Amsworth. How could one house and one man be the cause of so much fear and doubt?

On the night of the party, Alexander dressed in the latest evening fashion of black tailcoat, stiff shirt-front and white cravat. When the earl stepped from the front door onto the drive, Samuel Brown was not ready with the carriage. Alexander went to the stables and found him asleep in the hay with Robert Louis Stevenson's *Treasure Island* opened across his chest.

"Get up, you lazy thing! We must be off!" Alexander woke up the startled driver.

Before long Alexander was dropped off at Battlecrease House. As he looked at the balcony and the tree, he laughed despite himself. Mr. Amsworth greeted him in his effusive way and the evening commenced in the same manner as the previous party.

"I am so glad that you could make it! You surely received my letter." Amsworth swiftly changed the subject. "A few days ago, my cook was annoyed because the ham he had bought a few days prior had gone missing! Also, the dogs were in quite a mood when I arrived home the night before! I think someone may have broken in, but why on earth would they only take a ham?"

"Possibly, but perhaps the ham was misplaced?" countered Alexander.

"Nay!" replied Amsworth, "Look here."

Amsworth then produced a luxurious scrap of black

cloth. It was the ripped piece of Archambeau's coat! However, Alexander never knew about the ripped coat. But he had suspicions, due to his knowledge of Archambeau's fashion sense and the black coat he wore the night of the break-in.

"My gardener found this in the flower bed outside the back door! Someone broke into my home!"

"Well! Indeed, it appears so!" Alexander feigned surprise.

As Mr. Amsworth strutted away, Alexander remembered the real reason he was here. The earl scanned the party for an easy exit where he could explore more of the house without being noticed. He saw a break in the crowd, and meandered towards it, hoping not to be stopped. But alas! As Alexander was nearly to the door, he felt a thudding pat on the shoulder! It was Mr. Amsworth, who politely, yet sternly invited Alexander to the table.

The meal consisted of turkey, ham, rolls, vegetables, and more. Mr. Amsworth insisted he would carve the turkey and did so with perfect skill. Alexander was seated to the left of Amsworth, and tried his best to be entertaining and gracious, yet all the while thinking about how his strange host had almost surgically carved the turkey. It would make perfect sense, Alexander thought to himself, if Maybrick had been a cotton merchant, he must have been well learned with a blade, what with cutting fabrics to exact measurements, not to mention a needle and thread!

Learning from the mastery of Archambeau, Alexander made sure to take in his surroundings to the smallest detail. In doing so, he noticed that almost everyone (save the princess and a man at the other end of the table) were all present at the New Year's party. The unknown man at the other end of the table was sulking silently. A bear of a man, whose modest attire did little to hide his working-class background. Bulky and balding with massive arms, he would have been an intimidating figure in any scenario.

The party continued long into the night, much as it had on the previous occasion, and Alexander still failed to enter the forbidden rooms of the house. Consequently, when Samuel Brown slowed the carriage to a stop in front of the entrance, Alexander walked out with a look of disappointment on his face.

The next day, the young earl paid a visit to the home of Mr. Droves. Droves, wealthy as he may be, chose to live in a modest townhouse two blocks away from his factory. Alexander knocked on the door, and the French detective answered. Droves's maid presented the three with afternoon tea, as the crestfallen young man related to his accomplices the events of the night before.

"I could not leave the main rooms. Twice I tried to slip away, and twice I was flung back into the fray! Once by Amsworth himself, and once by a friend of his who I had not seen before and who proved an imposing figure." Alexander continued, "However, I can confirm with my own eyes the skill with which Mr. Amsworth carved the turkey. I suppose it is due to long hours of sewing and cutting fabrics, and such skills undoubtedly must have been implemented in his more gruesome activities. Also," Alexander exclaimed, waving his fork at Archambeau, "He told me about the break-in! He knew someone broke in and he has a scrap of fabric from your black coat!"

Archambeau replied coolly, "I do believe he confide

in you as a warning. I believe he knows more than he is letting on. I believe that, without the use of brutal tactics, which surely would soil our reputations, we may never see the underbelly of Battlecrease. That eliminates searching the house to find other organs from The Ripper's victims. This leaves us only one option: To locate and decipher the second letter of Mr. Goodborn!"

Droves interjected, saying: "But the secret letter was not hidden within the portrait, as Goodborn's letter described!"

"Perhaps we were searching in the wrong place. For the scene of the crime was Mr. Goodborn's summer estate. We must search his London home and perhaps find another painting. Perhaps the depiction of Uncle Roger in the Cotswolds was a duplication of an original work." Archambeau explained.

"Well, what are we waiting for?!" the earl exclaimed.

CHAPTER IX

The Warning

The following day began with wonderful news for Lord Shaftesbury. The princess had written a letter informing Alexander of her return to London. The young man could not have been happier. She was to arrive tomorrow morning on the 10:30 train at Paddington Station at platform 4. Alexander was greatly looking forward to seeing her again, but for now his focus was elsewhere. This morning, he was preparing to search Mr. Goodborn's home for the secret letter. He dressed in riding attire, and made sure to carry his pistol, a Webley-Pryse revolver which he had inherited from his father.

He rode alone on Moonlight to the home of Richard Goodborn. Archambeau was already waiting on the doorstep when Alexander arrived. In Goodborn's absence the butler, Mr. Lewis, was in charge. Mr. Lewis, although young and somewhat inexperienced, proved more than capable of carrying out the tasks which his title demanded

A rather reluctant Lewis granted them permission to search the house. To their surprise they found that the large, recently built home was being run as if Goodborn hadn't disappeared at all. The maids, cook, butler, and gardener were all still present.

The two split up as Alexander and Royce had done at Goodborn's Cotswolds home. The house was of an upper-class standard (although not on par with the grand estates with which Alexander was familiar). They searched the three stories, as well as the basement for portraits of Uncle Roger, along with other military depictions which may have some link to the late Lieutenant. In the house, they found several magnificent paintings. One was of a great charge on horseback and others were portraits of family members, but none held a letter within its canvas. After long hours of scrutinizing examination, the young earl and detective had produced nothing. Even the attic had no secrets to reveal. The day's search had resulted in disappointment, and the pair went their separate ways.

In the morning, the sun rose cheerfully, and the young Lord Shaftesbury did likewise. He instructed his valet that he wished to wear the morning suit with a blue brocade waist coat that he recently had made on Savile Row. He knew he would cut a dashing figure in the new costume, beaver top hat and leather gloves. Today marked the joyous arrival of Princess Romina.

Alexander found himself sitting near the fourth platform at Paddington station, awaiting her train. Soon he heard the screech of brakes as the great steam train came to a stop. He ood up and focused on the first-class carriages to better see the princess disembark. People filed out of the passenger cars. Some were tired and bedraggled and others excitedly fell into the arms of loved ones who had come to meet them. As the last few passengers descended onto platform 4, he had not seen her.

He stepped onto the train, and looked up and down the aisles, but his friend was nowhere to be seen! Panic welled up inside the young man, as he asked the conductor whether she had been on the list of passengers. Indeed, she was on the list in bold, with a note regarding a luxurious first-class car. Alexander wondered if perhaps she had gotten lost in the foreign Paddington Station. At once, the troubled earl began searching the platform and the surrounding area. In the mob of people, Alexander would never be able to identify a singular person. He ran back to the train, and back to the princess's first-class car. It was there he saw an envelope. It read, "Lord A.H. Shaftesbury III" in fancy script.

Alexander recognized the handwriting instantly, and a feeling of dread attacked his senses. Leaving the train, he slowly lowered himself onto a bench near the platform, and opened the grim letter, which read:

> *Good Friend, your inquisitive tendencies have not escaped my attention. I believe you were involved, however distantly, in the recent break-in at Mr. Amsworth's home. I have allowed this letter to fall into your hands, so that you may be warned. Your friend, the Frenchman, has delved too deeply into my affairs, and must cease his investigation of my own person if you ever wish to see your*

Russian friend again. If M. Archambeau has not returned to Paris within the week, your little confidante will join Miss Eddowes and the rest.

-Your Old Mate, Jack

CHAPTER X

The Frenchman's Departure

Alexander hastened back to Glamford then rode Moonlight to Droves's house in London. There he found Droves and the detective in the middle of an intellectual battle of chess. Alexander simply threw the letter onto the table, scattering the chess pieces to the floor. Picking up the missive, the inspector, dressed in his usual black coat and hat, read the letter. In response he simply winked and smiled at the young man. Without a word, he rose from his chair, strode to the front door, opened the door to leave and sauntered down the street. Alexander was left speechless.

As Alexander and Droves remain at the house, we will follow the footsteps of Archambeau, which lead us through the cramped London streets to a disreputable local tavern, whose bullet-riddled wooden sign above the door identifies it as Bolden's Pub. Mr. Henry Bolden had gained ownership of the pub back in the winter of 1868, after his father (the original founder of the establishment) had been slain in a duel two doors down in the back alley of Mr. Whitworth's Glass-Blowing Shop.

The young Henry didn't have his father's business acumen and soon experienced financial difficulties. Instead of losing the pub, he entered into a silent partnership with Goodborn Enterprises. Henry remained the public face of the pub, but behind the scenes the disreputable arm of Goodborn Enterprises implemented business practices to bring in more revenue and cheat unsuspecting patrons. Bolden's Pub was circumspectly avoided by the likes of Mr. Droves and other respectable businessmen. Instead, it was frequented by the more uncivilized members of the London docks area. Bolden's was a ramshackle little hole in the wall, and was always packed to the gills with sailors, scallywags, factory workers, and the old salts who told wild stories to anyone who would listen.

As Archambeau strode coolly through the door, he surveyed the area with his ever-watchful gaze. Many of the men studied the Frenchman discreetly, noticing the luxurious make of his garments and wondering about his identity. The detective approached the bar. The bartender whose name was long forgotten was simply known as "Niner", because he was missing the thumb on his left hand. Niner claimed to have lost the bet and his thumb in a high-stakes game of cards.

Archambeau ordered himself a drink and took a seat at the bar. By this time, most everyone in the place was murmuring amongst themselves about the strange man sitting at the bar. Superciliously sipping his drink, the detective continued surveying the pub and heard yelling from the dimly lit corner of the bar. Rising, he walked over to the ruckus and chuckled, "I knew I'd find him here," he thought to himself. There in the corner was DuMont, Archambeau's driver. M. DuMont was having the same good luck he previously experienced in the Cotswolds. He had gambled his way into a nice pile of coin, thus making the three rough looking men at the table very angry. Laughing nervously, DuMont looked over his shoulder and nearly dropped his cards when he saw his employer standing over him.

"Desolé copains, looks like it is time to go! Au revoir!" Du Mont said with a sarcastic laugh.

"Not so fast!" The bigger, bearded man stood up. "Where's our money, you rat!"

"Really I must be going!" DuMont said, growing more skittish by the second.

"The devil you are!" the bearded man said, reaching for the gun at his side.

BANG! In a split second, the man keeled over in pain, clutching his right arm. Everyone in the pub turned their heads to see Archambeau return his smoking revolver to its holster and begin to walk out. As he was departing, he threw a few shillings at Niner. He heard two clicks behind him. The other two men had risen from their chairs and were pointing their guns at the detective while his back was turned.

"You hold it right there!" one of them said.

Archambeau dropped his ivory handled revolver to the floor, and slowly turned to face them.

"I really am in a frightful hurry," the detective explained. "I came to fetch my driver, and I will allow you gentlemen to live, if you simply allow me to depart without any trouble."

"You don't got yer gun and yer tellin' US what to do?! I don't know 'bout you, but I ain't lettin' this fancy pants Frenchman boss me around," one of them cried in outrage.

At this, in the blink of an eye, the detective drew his second revolver from within his coat and shot a hole through the man's hand, causing him to yell and drop his gun. The other gambler dropped his gun to the floor and put his hands up. The detective then holstered both pistols with an entertaining flourish as DuMont pocketed the money that was lying on the table. Archambeau rolled his eyes at DuMont. He flashed his Parisian inspector's badge at Niner and voiding further altercation, he and DuMont slid into the narrow streets of London.

The next morning, a man in a black cloak and a magnificent, feathered hat stepped onto a passenger ship headed across the English Channel to Normandy. He flashed a badge and his papers as he boarded. As the man in the dark coat settled in, the ship blew its horn, and departed for the coast of northern France. That same morning, a man in London, outside the home of Charles Droves, was twisting his mustache as he filled a trough with water for his two horses and considered stopping by a pub after the day's work to play some cards.

The following day back at Glamford Castle, a much-relieved Alexander greeted the princess and her entourage. Mrs. Peters, the housekeeper, showed the princess's lady's maid to the servants' quarters, while Alexander directed the princess and her companion to their suite. Despite Alexander's countless questions, the princess was evasive and wished to keep the details of her detainment to herself.

Although she made it clear she wanted to stay at Glamford Castle where she felt safe in his protection. Throughout the day, the two went riding, walked in the garden and listened to the princess's companion play the pianoforte.

The fabled grandfather clock in the great hall struck midnight just as the princess retired to her suite. Not ready to retire, Lord Shaftesbury dozed off reclining in a lounge chair with a drink still in hand. He awoke a few minutes later. Still sleepy, his eyes focused on the reflection in the window. He thought he saw the figure of a man in the doorway behind him. Yet, when he turned his head to look no one was there. He shook his head, set his drink on the table beside him and promptly dozed off again.

The following three days were joyous. The two young people were inseparable. The couple lived lavishly. Alexander took the princess into London to see plays and eat at fancy restaurants (often at the recommendation of Chef Remmy). Alexander had forgotten about Mr. Amsworth entirely. But one evening while returning from the theater a light rain fell. Per usual, the princess and her companion retired first. Later, Alexander made his way through the great hall on his way to the staircase. While passing the floor to ceiling windows that lined the great hall, he noticed the patterns of rain on the moonlit windows. The moonlight also cast shadows on the floor. As he walked along, he noticed something odd. One window cast a different shadow than the rest. Alexander glanced up, only to see the outline of a man in the window! Startled, the young earl jumped back! Suddenly, a great boom of thunder shook the room. When Alexander looked again, the shadow was gone!

CHAPTER XI

Uncle Roger's Secret

The next day, Alexander decided not to worry the princess with his odd experience. However, he did ask her once again for details on where she was held captive. The only thing she would say was that a man, fitting the description of the big burly man from the party, had been the architect behind the scheme. She had described being blindfolded for the entirety of her captivity. Once the princess had left, Alexander headed to Droves's house. When Samuel Brown dropped the earl off at the factory owner's home, he was greeted at the door by Droves's driver.

"Hello Inspector! So, you have made it back to France with no complications?" asked Alexander.

"I have indeed executed my plan perfectly! The only tragedy is that I must be seen in these vêtements pauvres!" the inspector complained. "But I believe I am the only man in history to be in two countries at once! I gave my driver, M. DuMont, my papers, coat and hat, and sent him to Paris where he shall pose as myself. But, here in London I remain to carry on my investigation under the guise of the driver for M. Droves! Condamner these rags!"

Alexander and Samuel Brown laughed hysterically at the disgusted inspector's predicament while Alexander began to explain the reason why he had come to see Mr. Droves.

"I believe I have made an important discovery! Late at night, I was re-reading the letter from Mr. Goodborn when I noticed a flaw in our interpretation! The letter only stated that a secret was to be found "inside of Uncle Roger" NOT specifically inside of a painting!"

"Quite clever, Lord Shaftesbury! You may be a detective yet!" Archambeau applauded. "Do you mean to infer that Mr. Goodborn wrote the letter with quite a more literal meaning than we previously assumed?! That perhaps the second note is with Uncle Roger himself?!"

"Then we must recover this letter at once!" exclaimed Mr. Droves.

"Especially since I believe to have seen a man at my home at Glamford for the past couple nights! Probably a spy of Amsworth's, or worse, Amsworth himself! We must get that letter before Amsworth finds it and destroys it, for it may be our only lead to finally capturing him!"

The friends spent the day researching Mr. Goodborn's family history. Past records showed many places where family members were buried. They debated through the day and planned through the night. The following evening, Alexander and Archambeau set off in Mr. Droves' carriage. Archambeau posed as Lord Shaftesbury's driver, and the two headed to a small white church near the stately home of

Mr. Goodborn. This time, Alexander was dressed in black. As for Archambeau, he begrudgingly wore the working-class attire fitting of a humble carriage driver. The two searched the cemetery that was beside the little white church. It was a cold, clear, windless night, and the moon was full. An owl hooted in a nearby gnarled old tree. The shadows of the night danced across the gravestones of the dead. The two compatriots kept searching for a grave, until Alexander hissed, "Come here! I've found it!"

Archambeau came to the very back of the cemetery, where Alexander was standing over the grave of the one and only Lt. Roger Goodborn! Alexander waited by the grave while the inspector retrieved a pair of shovels from the carriage located near the church. When he returned, he kept watch while Alexander started digging. As Alexander continued digging, the once light breeze intensified. The wind whistled with an eeriness and an owl hooted ominously in a nearby tree. The baleful howl of a distant dog was distorted by the wind, as if to warn them, "do not disturb the dead". The night gradually grew colder and more bitter. Alexander kept digging.

Alexander's shovel unexpectedly struck a hard surface! Archambeau abandoned his post and rushed over in excitement to see what had happened. As Alexander swept away debris with his hands, he realized the hard surface was the lid of a coffin. It was a simple wooden coffin with no ornamentation. The detective helped Alexander wrestle the coffin out of the hole. They looked at each other excitedly as they gently pried it open. This coffin could contain the all-important clue! Inside, they discovered the gruesome remains of Uncle Roger! Clutched in his skeletal fingers was a letter!

Alexander could not wait! He opened the letter and read it aloud to Archambeau!

Dear Friend,

You have found my second letter! Indeed, it was with Uncle Roger, as I said. Due to the revelations contained in this letter, I needed to hide it well. In my last letter, I mentioned the feeling of peril that has attached itself to my soul. This peril goes by the name of Jack the Ripper. Last month, I attended a party at the home of a cotton merchant, but that man had passed, and his relative had taken up residence. His relative was a Mr. J. Kirby Amsworth. He and I had gotten into a deep discussion about finance and my factory. He very much wanted to do business with me and went so far as to propose a partnership! I declined his offer. It was after that party that I started feeling uneasy. At my home, I saw shadows at night, and sometimes the figure of a man sitting in another room. Admittedly, I am quite fond of the bottle, so I passed it off as nothing; thinking I had had one scotch too many. But then the letter came. It was written in red ink, and it held threats to my life if I did not sell my London linens factory. Even more disturbing was the human ear that was sent to me in the following days. Both letters were signed, "from Hell". I need help. This monster, I assume, must be related to the man from the party. If they are in cahoots, I have one possible way to stop them. When I was at the party, I wandered around the house and found myself in an empty room. This empty room had a fireplace, and I recognized it as like my own. It was of the same make. The fireplace in my estate has a little latch that causes it to spin round and situate you in a secret room. I believe that the fireplace in that empty room was also built with the same feature. Good luck! I will surely perish within the month, but I implore you to avenge me!

Richard Harold Goodborn
19 December 1891

After reading the letter, Archambeau exclaimed, "My God! This could be the evidence we need! We must attempt a second break-in! Whatever may be behind that false fireplace will surely be the nail in the coffin of M. Amsworth!"

Just then, a deep voice said, "London Police! Don't move, you are under arrest!"

CHAPTER XII

Help Comes in a Tweed Suit

Newgate Prison was located at the corner of Newgate Street and Old Bailey Street in London. Once an imposing sight, the prison had fallen into disrepair. Overcrowded and underfunded, it was an inhumane cesspit of murderers, burglars, and gangsters. Archambeau and Alexander sat in their dank cell and thought. They had already examined their surroundings. The walls were old, but not old enough to be weakened. The cell door was forged iron. And should they escape their cell, they still had to get past the intimidating prison guards undetected. Two days passed, and the two spoke of possible methods of escape. They also had plenty of time to dream up a plan to get inside Battlecrease House. But their plans were for naught as long as they were imprisoned. The guards and keeper of the prison did not believe Alexander when he informed them that he was a member of the aristocracy. Archambeau's badge was with DuMont in Paris and consequently of no use.

To best utilize their time incarcerated, Archambeau drew a rough plan of Battlecrease House on the floor of the cell. They debated different methods to gain access to the house. Alexander's plan was to repeat their last attempt but silence the dogs this time. Archambeau believed unapologetic forced entry was necessary, until he remembered that his papers and Gendarmerie badge were in the possession of DuMont, who at this very moment was in Paris pretending to be him. As the two puzzled, they heard their cell door slide open with a loud screech. To their utter astonishment, next to the guard, stood the prison's head of security and Governor Arthur Royce!

Royce looked at the two and raised an eyebrow at Archambeau's outfit. In his most authoritative voice, Royce bellowed to the head of security, "Well! This is my London contact! You have arrested the wrong men! I sent them legally to recover important details concerning national security! This man is scheduled to travel to Cape Town in three days and you are holding him up!"

"And who is he?" asked the head of security, pointing to Archambeau.

"Er-" Royce began to stutter.

Quickly interrupting, the detective interjected, "Je suis son traducteur. I am his translator, for Monsieur was in London to speak at the French Embassy."

"Oh, I see…" the man said. "Well, Governor, I do sincerely apologize for such a mishap! I will write a scorching letter to the police for such a blunder!"

"I appreciate your understanding, sir! And I certainly

hope those grave robbers are caught and punished!" exclaimed Royce.

Alexander and Archambeau were silent as Royce led them out of Newgate Prison. Both men wondered at what had just transpired.

Governor Royce took them to his estate where Alexander and Archambeau ate their fill and recuperated. Both were happy to have real food after two days and nights of prison gruel. As they were eating, Royce recounted the events of his return.

"I do say! I had been led astray! I departed for Africa because I had received a letter from my associate saying I was urgently needed. But I soon found out that the letter was faked! And my associate's signature was forged! Since the Muskoka was a merchant ship there were no other passengers, save myself.

"When I boarded the Muskoka, Captain Rubio greeted me personally and treated me like a king. The captain was too affable and accommodating. I became more and more suspicious so, I started a little investigation! While I was in the captain's cabin for supper one evening (a type of invitation never, in my experience, proffered), he stepped out to check a heading with the first mate. I took this opportunity to search through the papers scattered about the chart table. Among several of the charts and papers were notes from none other than Mr. Amsworth! It turns out, the captain was paid by Mr. Amsworth to get rid of me!

"When the captain realized I had caught onto his scheme, he threw me in the brig! As you might imagine, this was a most unpleasant arrangement! Rats regularly visited my cell to steal food! The cabin boy, whom I had met prior to my imprisonment, was charged with bringing food and water to me daily. Billy Clarke was a bright young lad who had been abducted near the wharf while running an errand for his mum. We quickly became friends because I was kind to him. He was grossly mistreated and beaten by the captain and crew. To spite his captors, he was kind enough to provide information about what was happening above deck. The lad advised me that we were headed southwest and would land on the island of Carib within a week.

"The week passed. On that Saturday, we were caught in a mighty storm! The wind howled and waves crashed over the deck. I was thrown about my cell and believed myself a goner. As you know, I am not prone to sea sickness, but I am ashamed to say that I was quite ill. My cell, which was at the bottom of the ship, took on water. Even the rats evacuated to higher decks. The ship nearly capsized! The captain managed to beach our ship on a sandbar near shore.

"He ordered his crew to bind my hands and feet with rope and we rowed ashore in rough seas. They forced me into a small tent where I was guarded day and night. I knew that I had to escape and get back to you as soon as possible! So, I took a chance! At night when everyone was asleep, I rolled to the back of the tent and commenced digging a hole in the sand with my hands. I thought I would never make the hole large enough for me to fit through, given my size and that my wrists and ankles were bound, but by Jove I did! I wriggled my way out to the other side, where I proceeded to roll away."

"WHAT?!" cried Alexander in disbelief, "What happened next?!"

"Well, I rolled as far as I could that night. It was too dark to see anything, but I kept rolling farther and farther until I was exhausted and fell asleep. When I awoke the next morning, I found myself looking at the entrance to a cave somewhere along the beach. So naturally, I rolled myself into the cave. I freed my hands by rubbing the rope against a sharp, protruding rock and untied my feet. I explored the cave but found nothing.

"I spent the day collecting the few coconuts I could find. I returned to the cave and let go of my pile, and one coconut rolled down a crevice I had not previously noticed! When I reached down, to retrieve the coconut...much to my astonishment, I found that it was not a coconut I held. It was a golden bowl!"

"Impossible!" Archambeau nearly spit out his food.

"Not such a crazy story as it may seem!" In his usual story-telling manner, Royce continued, hardly pausing to take a breath. "For in that crevice was a massive stash of gold! Doubloons, goblets, candlesticks, and more! And I remembered that this was not Carib! We had obviously been blown off course. As I was collecting this gold, I suddenly recalled a story Alexander's grandfather had told me. It was a story about a pirate named Red Robert, who was a long-ago relative! I could only assume we had landed on one of The Seven Isles, and I unwittingly found the lost treasure of Red Robert!

"Under the cover of darkness, I stole one of the lifeboats and snuck off the island. I floated aimlessly on the sea for more than a day before an American naval vessel spotted me and came to my rescue. The American Navy and I returned to the island to arrest my captors and free my young friend, Billy Clarke. By-the-by, it turns out that Billy loves the sea now and when he returns home to England, he will join the Royal Navy. As for the treasure, I brought a small chest back with me, and the rest of the treasure is being transported on an English warship."

Alexander and Archambeau looked stunned. "How can you be certain that it was Robert's treasure?" asked Archambeau.

"I am certain we can confirm it!" Royce went on, "Hidden away with the gold was the small chest I brought with me. And to every chest, there must be a key!"

"That means that if one of us has the key to that chest, then you DID find Red Robert's treasure!" exclaimed an excited Alexander. "And thanks to Archambeau, I know where it is!"

CHAPTER XIII

The Secret Room

Alexander rose from the table and beckoned Royce and the inspector to come with him. They took Royce's carriage to Glamford Castle, and Alexander led them to Sir Percival's study.

"I would have long forgotten this room if it were not for you, Inspector. You found it once again during your break-in at Christmas and later reminded me of the War Room when you brought Droves and me down here."

The owner of The Seven Isles lit a small table lamp and pulled out the big red book that was on the shelf nearest the outer wall. He led Archambeau and his amazed godfather down into Red Robert's secret room.

They looked around the small space orienting themselves in the dim light. Royce had not been in the dugout shelter since his younger days with Alexander's father. Alexander lit more candles while Royce set the small chest on the center table. Alexander opened the large chest that was in the corner of the shelter. He rummaged around, gently moving aside a bloodstained Union Jack; a decorative, yet grungy coat of the Royal Navy; a battered Tricorn hat; and Red Robert's personal journal and captain's log. Finally, his hand rested on the object he was seeking, a brass key!

Alexander fit the key to the lock of the small chest that now rested on the center table. Slowly turning the key, the latch sprung open! He lifted the lid, reached in the chest removing its sole content: A yellowed paper, signed by King William III. It was the privateer's commission given to Red Robert!

"By Jove!" Royce exclaimed. "It IS the lost treasure!"

After a self-congratulatory celebration, the trio decided a new plan was in order. Since Royce had captured Amsworth's accomplices, Archambeau could use them as a connection to capture Amsworth!

The following morning, the trio paid a visit to the City of London's Chief of Police, Ernest Ellis. The chief was a portly man with a graying mustache who had, through years of tough work, risen to the commanding role he now filled. And fill it he did. He was not known to back down or give up on a case. His dogged determination, and strict, stern way of motivating his officers had proven successful throughout his years in command.

Royce gave the chief the details of his capture and explained how Mr. Amsworth connected to his imprisonment. Archambeau then introduced himself and gave the chief an account of his discoveries in the Jack the Ripper case. As he listened, Ellis became agitated.

Unbeknownst to the trio, the chief had three years

earlier been assigned to Frederick George Abberline who was the chief investigator on the Jack the Ripper case. Ellis was present when Mr. George Lusk delivered the gruesome kidney and letter from Jack the Ripper to the Commercial Street Police Station. The unsolved Jack the Ripper case was a sorry blot on his career. If Amsworth really was Jack the Ripper, he was determined that this rat be brought to justice!

That evening, the chief sent three officers and a patrol wagon to arrest Mr. Amsworth for attempted murder, and unlawfully assisting a criminal in the Governor Royce abduction. They would also have the opportunity to further investigate and cross examine Amsworth regarding the Ripper murders! Alexander, Archambeau, and Royce fervently requested that they accompany the policemen to the arrest. The officers knocked on the door of Battlecrease House, but nobody answered. When the officers broke down the door, they saw that the house was empty. At almost the same moment a shot rang out. One of the officers collapsed to the ground, clutching his leg! The other two officers spotted a dark figure dashing across the street. The figure stopped and fire again, killing the second officer. The third officer ran to the aid of his fallen comrade. It seemed that Amsworth would escape!

CHAPTER XIV

The East End

Mr. Amsworth doubled back to his stable, mounted a saddled horse and galloped off. The chase was on! Fortunately, Alexander had ridden to the house on Moonlight, and chased Amsworth through the streets! Amsworth occasionally fired a shot at Alexander, who fired back with his father's old pistol! Amsworth tried to elude Alexander as he weaved up and down the precarious streets. They ended up in the narrow streets of London's East End. The Whitechapel district, to be exact!

Amsworth's horse could not navigate the narrow streets…so he hopped off and ran. Alexander stayed atop Moonlight, and carefully patrolled the dodgy streets. Soon Royce and Archambeau caught up, and the three left their horses, and walked side-by-side down the main street, pistols drawn, checking dark doorways and alleys. Amsworth could be anywhere and ready to pounce.

The clouds that had been looming over London all day

finally began to speak. As heavy rain fell the sky darkened into night. Pedestrians began seeking shelter from the rain, clearing the streets. An occasional boom of thunder, followed by the crack of lightning, intensified the view of their surroundings. The trio continued their march searching for the infamous killer. Now drenched, they turned up their collars and ignored the cold and biting wind. Alexander was in his expensive riding outfit and spurred boots, Royce in his tweed suit with his tan bowler hat firmly fixed on his head, and Archambeau once again in a black coat, black leather boots and wide brimmed hat. The three walked calmly and slowly down the street, hoping to draw The Ripper from his hiding place. They kept searching; the storm kept raging. Then, after a bright crack of lightning, they saw a solitary figure ahead of them.

POW! A shot rang out, and Arthur Royce dropped to the ground. Archambeau fired back, but the figure had vanished! Alexander yelled and rushed to his godfather's aid, only to see that the shot was fatal. The young earl picked up Royce's old revolver and kept moving forward with Archambeau to his right. Alexander had no time to grieve, but anger welled up inside of him.

BOOM! Another crack of thunder. The two compatriots kept walking. Archambeau with his ivory-handled revolvers at the ready, and Alexander with his father's revolver in one hand, and Royce's old, worn revolver in the other.

The figure appeared again, but this time so far down the road that Alexander could barely see him. Their deliberate pace turned into a run, as Alexander and the French detective charged after Amsworth! The younger Alexander ran faster than Archambeau and he started catching up to the fleeing Amsworth! Meanwhile, Archambeau ran down an alleyway and climbed a ladder leading to the rooftops. Alexander played a game of cat and mouse with Amsworth through the streets of the East End, until the two met in a narrow alleyway.

"Give yourself up, Amsworth!" Alexander yelled.

"Royce isn't here to save you now!" Amsworth sneered. "Before I kill you, I will answer one question!"

"He isn't here because you killed him!" Alexander yelled, "Are you Jack the Ripper?"

"I AM!" yelled Amsworth with pride. "And nobody will ever know!" Amsworth started to laugh maniacally, "After I kill you, I will disappear! No one will find me, and nobody will remember you!"

As Amsworth was about to raise his gun, two shots rang out! The man claiming to be Jack the Ripper was dead. Two bullets went through his heart! Alexander dropped his guns and looked up. On the roof above the alley was Inspector Gerard Archambeau, his ivory-handled revolvers still smoking, and his black coat waving in the wind.

The next morning, police entered the house on 7 Riversdale Road, and began a thorough search. Accompanying those policemen were Alexander and Archambeau, who directed them according to the details of Goodborn's second letter. And indeed, when Alexander kicked a protruding brick in the fireplace, it spun round, placing the young earl inside a small room. In this secret room was none other than Richard Goodborn! Goodborn was in a bad way. He was much diminished in comparison to his former self, and consequently humbled. Goodborn had lost weight and had dark circles under his eyes. Although he was in poor health, the sight of rescue brought a resurgence of life into the wealthy man's features.

Alexander quickly untied Mr. Goodborn and checking for wounds, Alexander determined that Goodborn was only dehydrated and starved. They lead the captive from his prison into the outer room. Once he had drank some water and eaten, Goodborn recounted the details of his story and disappearance.

"Thank God! You must have found my letter! I had to hide it somewhere no one would expect. Somewhere outside of the house. Quite a lot has happened since I was captured, and captured I was! I had been receiving letters threatening my life if I did not give Amsworth ownership of my London factory. The author was quite grotesque in his choice of diction.

'After the second threat, I was seriously afraid for my life. I decided to write and hide my letters, hoping someone would find them. On the night of 22 December, two men entered my room and gagged me! I lost consciousness and when I awoke, I was bound in that secret room and bolted to the floor! I was still able to hear what was happening in the outer room. I overheard some intense discussions during my detainment, most of which I don't understand."

"What did you hear? Perhaps we may be able to shed some light on the subject?" Alexander asked.

"Well," Goodborn continued, "I overheard Amsworth speaking to someone in the room outside, during what must have been a party. He mentioned something about Carib, and I also heard him ask if someone had found it yet."

Archambeau, deep in thought, started pacing and twirling his mustache. "If what you say is true, then it is all connected! Royce told us that he was captured on a ship that was headed for Carib, a small island in the Caribbean. But they were blown off course and landed on one of Alexander's Seven Isles. It was there that Royce accidentally found a lost treasure. Treasure belonging to one of Alexander's ancestors. It is my opinion that the crew of the ship, hired by Amsworth, was looking for that treasure!"

"But why would Amsworth try to find the treasure, and how did he know about it?" asked a bewildered Goodborn.

"To buy your company!" replied Alexander. "Once owning your company as well as his own, he would be perpetually wealthy and could live in anonymity. No one would suspect a thing! Amsworth had been creeping around my home for weeks before I discovered it. He must have found the hidden cellar. It was there that he learned about my pirate relative, Red Robert, and his lost treasure. He wanted control of your company to expand his failing merchant business. With the treasure he would be independently wealthy and could simply buy your company. It was a perfect front for an anonymous life of luxury. But his crew had their sights on the wrong island, Carib, and due to a storm accidentally land on the REAL island!"

After hearing this, Goodborn was astounded. The three men and the police left the house on 7 Riversdale Road and Mr. Goodborn was taken to his physician for a thorough examination before returning to his home. The police would gather his full statement once he had recovered. Alexander mounted Moonlight and returned to Glamford Castle where the princess anxiously awaited his return. Archambeau saluted the gentlemen and climbed into his waiting brougham carriage. DuMont dutifully whipped up the horse as they disappeared into the late afternoon light.

EPILOGUE

The following week, Arthur Royce was laid to rest. In his will, he left his estate to Alexander, who had also received Red Robert's treasure, a portion of which he gave to Archambeau. Inspector Gerard Archambeau became a hero throughout Europe for his efforts and finally accomplished his dream of becoming the most famous detective in the world. He went back to Paris and lived in luxury. As for Amsworth, it was discovered that he was indeed Mr. Maybrick, and that he had been guilty of capturing Royce, as well as attempted murder. Much as detectives tried, Maybrick was never actually proven to be Jack the Ripper.

One month after that fateful stormy night in London, a young earl married a beautiful princess. They had a son, named Jonathan Royce Shaftesbury, who would one day have his own adventures.

Although the London police were still searching for Jack the Ripper, London could breathe freely once again… at least for a little while. On the horizon were other conflicts after which the world would never be the same.

But that is not quite the end of our story…

One hundred years later, in a pub in Liverpool, a diary

changed hands. Given to a scrap metal worker, this diary was supposedly found under the floorboards of an old house on 7 Riversdale Road. It has yet to be proven legitimate by today's historians, who, along with the vast majority of the population, are still baffled by the mysterious case of Jack the Ripper. However, those of you who now know this tale, may have just read how things really happened over one hundred years ago…

THE END

CHARACTERS OF FICTION

Alexander Horatio Shaftesbury III: 17th Earl of Glamford

Arthur Royce: Alexander's Godfather, Governor of S. African Colony

Gerard Archambeau: Famous French Detective

Princess Romina Casinova: Russian Princess

Richard Goodborn: Wealthy Factory Owner

Charles Droves: Wealthy Factory Owner

Kirby Amsworth: Relative of James Maybrick

Samuel Brown: Alexander's Driver and Stableboy

Pierre DuMont: Gerard Archambeau's Driver and Lackey

Rene DuBlanc: Alexander's Personal Chef

Walter Billingsby: Alexander's Butler

Madame Gertrude Plum: Neighbor and Local Gossip

Gordon Hammond: Glamford Castle Groundskeeper

Captain Rubio: Captain, Merchant Vessel Muskoka

Billy Clarke: Cabin boy, Merchant Vessel Muskoka

Ernest Ellis: London Chief of Police

Jonathan Royce Shaftesbury: Son of Alexander and Princess Romina

CHARACTERS OF HISTORY

Jack the Ripper: Unidentified serial killer believed responsible for at least five 1888 murders, in and around the Whitechapel district of London, England.

James Maybrick: Deceased Merchant***

Frederick George Abberline: Chief Investigator on the Jack the Ripper Case

George Lusk: Chairman of the Whitechapel Vigilance Committee

*1874 would be the last year for outstanding Bordeaux wine until at least 1891. Between 1875 and 1892 there was an aphid phylloxera outbreak that destroyed entire vineyards throughout most of Europe. Eventually the vines were saved by grafting Bordeaux scions onto American rootstock that could resist the disease.

**Sir Francis Galton was an early pioneer in the 1880s, studying how fingerprints were unique and constant throughout a person's lifetime. A police officer in Argentina used Galton's research to identify a murderer in 1892.

***James Maybrick is rumored to have been Jack the Ripper, along with a few other suspects. Maybrick lived in the Battlecrease House until his mysterious death. He is believed to have been murdered by his wife, and the Ripper murders stopped shortly after his death in May 1889.

Printed in the United States
by Baker & Taylor Publisher Services